Hello, Family Members,

Learning to read is one of the most important accomplishments of early childhood. **Hello Reader!** books help children become skilled readers who like to read. Beginning readers learn to read by remembering frequently used words like "the," "is," and "and"; by using phonics skills to decode new words; and by interpreting picture and text clues. These books provide both the stories children enjoy and the structure they need to read fluently and independently. Here are suggestions for helping your child *before*, *during*, and *after* reading:

Before
- Look at the cover and pictures and have your child predict what the story is about.
- Read the story to your child.
- Encourage your child to chime in with familiar words and phrases.
- Echo read with your child by reading a line first and having your child read it after you do.

During
- Have your child think about a word he or she does not recognize right away. Provide hints such as "Let's see if we know the sounds" and "Have we read other words like this one?"
- Encourage your child to use phonics skills to sound out new words.
- Provide the word for your child when more assistance is needed so that he or she does not struggle and the experience of reading with you is a positive one.
- Encourage your child to have fun by reading with a lot of expression . . . like an actor!

After
- Have your child keep lists of interesting and favorite words.
- Encourage your child to read the books over and over again. Have him or her read to brothers, sisters, grandparents, and even teddy bears. Repeated readings develop confidence in young readers.
- Talk about the stories. Ask and answer questions. Share ideas about the funniest and most interesting characters and events in the stories.

I do hope that you and your child enjoy this book.

—Francie Alexander
Chief Education Officer,
Scholastic's Learning Ventures

For Justin Thomas

— *M.P.*

For Stasia, the Pickle Princess

— *G.U.*

Go to scholastic.com for web site information on
Scholastic authors and illustrators.

ISBN 0-439-32094-1

Copyright © 2002 by Nancy Hall, Inc.
All rights reserved. Published by Scholastic Inc.
SCHOLASTIC, HELLO READER, CARTWHEEL BOOKS, and associated logos
are trademarks and/or registered trademarks of Scholastic Inc.

Library of Congress Cataloging-in-Publication Data

Packard, Mary.
  The missing tooth / by Mary Packard; illustrated by George Ulrich.
  p. cm. – (Hello reader! Level 1)
  "Cartwheel books."
  Summary: Rhyming tale of a first-grade girl waiting to lose her first tooth so that
she will have a spacey smile just like all her classmates.
  ISBN 0-439-32094-1 (pbk.)
  [1.—Fiction. 2. Schools—Fiction. 3. Stories in rhyme.]
  I. Ulrich, George, ill. II. Title. III. Series.
  PZ8.3 +
  [E] — dc21   2001032264

10 9 8 7 6   03   04   05   06
                            Printed in the U.S.A.
                        First printing, February 2002

The Missing Tooth

by Mary Packard
Illustrated by George Ulrich

Hello Reader! — Level 1

SCHOLASTIC INC.

New York   Toronto   London   Auckland   Sydney
Mexico City   New Delhi   Hong Kong   Buenos Aires

I had a big problem.
I was just so upset!
None of my teeth
had fallen out yet.

I checked out my teeth,
top and bottom each night.
Not one tooth was loose.
Each one was in tight.

In school I would give
each tooth a good nudge.
It just was no use.
My teeth did not budge.

A mouth filled with teeth
makes you feel like a fool.
You see, in first grade,
spacey smiles are so cool.

Max lost his front tooth
when he played hide-and-seek.

And Jen lost her tooth
in an apple last week.

Then this morning at breakfast
my tooth just popped out!

I jumped off my chair
and let out a shout.

"Hey, Mom! Hey, Dad!
Look what happened!" I said.

"My tooth just fell out
when I bit down on my bread!"

I felt with my tongue
where my tooth used to be.
It felt empty and strange—
and just perfect to me!

I showed off my gap
when I got on the bus.
And even the driver
made a big fuss!

When I got to school
it took quite a while
to show everyone there
my new spacey smile.

At the end of the day,
I saw Grandma Ruth.
"Hi, sweetheart," she said.
"Will you show me your tooth?"

I reached into my pocket.
"Sure, Grandma," I said.

But my tooth wasn't there—
just a big hole instead!

We searched and we searched.
We looked all around.
But hard as we tried,
my tooth couldn't be found!

I got ready for bed
and much to my shock—
there was my tooth
tumbling out of my sock!

It had slipped through my pocket,
not making a sound,
and dropped into my sock.
Hooray! It was found!

So I got into bed
and turned out the light.
And the best part of all—
it was tooth fairy night!